Garry Chapman

eXtreme SPORTS

SNOW

WARNING:

Extreme sports can be very dangerous. Mishaps can result in death or serious injury.
Seek expert advice before attempting any of the stunts you read about in this book.

This book is for Greg, Noelene, Hayley, Shelley and Jessica Madge.

This edition first published in 2002 in the United States of America by Chelsea House Publishers, a subsidiary of Haights Cross Communications.

Chelsea House Publishers
1974 Sproul Road, Suite 400
Broomall, PA 19008-0914

The Chelsea House world wide web address is www.chelseahouse.com

Library of Congress Cataloging-in-Publication Data Applied for.

ISBN 0-7910-6607-X

First published in 2001 by
Macmillan Education Australia Pty Ltd
627 Chapel Street, South Yarra, Australia, 3141

Copyright © Garry Chapman 2001

Edited by Renée Otmar, Otmar Miller Consultancy Pty Ltd
Text design by if design
Cover design by if design
Printed in China

J
796.6
CHA

Acknowledgements
The author and the publisher are grateful to the following for permission to reproduce copyright material:

Cover photo of ski-boarder courtesy of Allsport/Mike Powell.

Allsport, pp. 25, 27 (top), 29; Allsport/Mike Powell, pp. 16–17, 22, 23, 24, 26–28; Australian Picture Library/Corbis, pp. 6–7; Australian Picture Library/Fotopic, p. 13; Australian Picture Library/Picture Box, p. 14; Getty Images, pp. 9, 12; PhotoDisc, pp. 8, 16 (insert), 30; Sport. The Library, p. 11; Sport. The Library/Andrew Barnes, p. 10; Sport. The Library/Bill Bachman, pp. 4 (bottom), 6–7 (insert); Sport. The Library/Chris McLennan, pp. 4–5; Sport. The Library/Jeff Crow, pp. 14–15, 19; Sport. The Library/Tony Harrington, pp. 18 (top), 20, 21.

While every care has been taken to trace and acknowledge copyright the publishers tender their apologies for any accidental infringement where copyright has proved untraceable.

Contents

Winter in the Snow **4**

Playground for snow sports enthusiasts 4

Taking snow sports to extremes 5

Destination Snow **6**

Ski resorts 6

Skiing in the southern hemisphere 6

Skiing in the northern hemisphere 7

Gear Up for the Snow **8**

Safety in the Snow **10**

Snowboarding **12**

Freeriding 14

Freestyle and Boardercross 16

Free Skiing **18**

Free Skiing at Valdez 20

Skiboarding **22**

Skiboard Fun 24

Snow Mountain Biking **26**

Biker X 28

Snow Jargon **30**

Glossary **31** Index 32

PLAYGROUND FOR SNOW SPORTS ENTHUSIASTS

It is winter. Snow falls on the steep mountain slopes, transforming them overnight into glistening white playgrounds for skiers and snowboarders. In anticipation of clear blue skies, fresh, untracked **powder** snow and spectacular alpine scenery, snow sports enthusiasts flock to ski **resorts** in search of challenge and excitement.

Fun for everyone

Ski slopes present different challenges to different people. Some people are content simply to throw snowballs or ride inflated tubes down gentle slopes. Other visitors to the snow yearn for a much greater element of risk and danger.

Skiing

Most skiers prefer to remain on **trails**, or within the bounds of the groomed snow on the marked ski runs. Daredevils like to venture off the trails into more remote areas, in search of solitude and adventure.

Snowboarding

Conventional skiers used to think of snowboarders as the rebels of the snowfields. Snowboarders seek the **adrenaline rush** that comes from **carving** huge turns or executing gravity defying flips and rotations.

Free skiing

Extreme, or free skiing, pits the adventurous skier against the mountain itself. The free skier's experience might include:

- ☞ **hurtling downhill at breakneck speeds**
- ☞ **narrowly avoiding treacherous rocks**
- ☞ **dropping several feet through the air from snowy cliffs**
- ☞ **carving through shoulder-deep powder snow.**

Winter fun at the Snowtubing Park at Australia's Mount Buller ski resort.

TAKING SNOW SPORTS TO EXTREMES

Traditional skiing and snowboarding are still the most popular of snow sports.

Xtreme Fact

Crested Butte in the Rocky Mountains, USA is a favorite skiing destination. It has hosted the United States extreme skiing titles and the Winter X Games. The resort receives an average of 550 centimeters (18 feet) of snow annually, and features some of the world's best lift-served extreme slopes.

Variations on traditional sports

By combining elements of established sports with the unique features of the snow environment, new sports evolve. Two recent extreme snow sports to emerge are snow mountain biking and skiboarding. Mountain bike racers discovered that their sport could be adapted easily to racing in snow. In order to race in the snow, they had to add studs to their bike tires and make a few adjustments to their riding style. Skiboarding came about when skiers abandoned their poles, shortened their skis and adopted the side-to-side movement previously associated with inline skating. Skiers and snowboarders continue to explore the many possibilities of the alpine terrain. As hi-tech equipment continues to improve, it is likely that more extreme versions of traditional snow sports will surface. Many of these new and exciting snow sports are now featured in the Winter X Games and similar competitions. Some are now even featured in the Winter Olympics every four years.

The risks and rewards

In order to enjoy the snow, skiers and boarders must be fit and must remain conscious of safety procedures. Extreme snow sports demand strength, flexibility, reserves of energy and a high level of aerobic fitness. High-speed tumbles can result in torn ligaments and broken limbs. The risks involved can be great, but the rewards can be even greater.

Destination Snow

SKI RESORTS

The most popular snow sports destinations are ski resorts. A resort is usually a township or village which has a lift system able to transport thousands of skiers and boarders each day to the top of the mountain. From there you can tackle the **terrain** best suited to your abilities. When snow is scarce, resort operators make their own snow, using the latest snow-making equipment available. This often allows them to open up additional ski runs and to extend the length of the ski season.

Challenging terrain

Extreme skiers and boarders favor areas with many varieties of challenging terrain. This includes steep runs down fast faces, spectacular scenery and lots of powder snow.

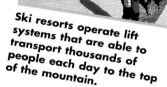

Ski resorts operate lift systems that are able to transport thousands of people each day to the top of the mountain.

SKIING IN THE SOUTHERN HEMISPHERE

Thredbo

In the southern hemisphere, the snow season runs from about June to September in both Australia and New Zealand. Thredbo, high in the Snowy Mountains, is arguably Australia's top ski resort. Much of the Thredbo terrain is fast and steep. In some places it is almost vertical. Free skiers and boarders can launch themselves into the air from any number of rock drops and natural tabletops. The runs are long, and are sure to get the adrenaline pumping.

Southern Alps

Close to Queenstown, on New Zealand's South Island, lie the Southern Alps. Ski regions in this range include Coronet Peak, Cardrona and Wanaka. Wanaka is the home of the annual Heli-Challenge, which gathers some of the world's most daring free skiers and extreme snowboarders for a spectacular three-day event.

SKIING IN THE NORTHERN HEMISPHERE

The European Alps

Snow generally comes to the northern hemisphere from about December to March. Snow falls throughout the Alps in Europe, where skiers and boarders can visit resorts in France, Italy, Austria and Switzerland.

Europe's highest cable car

Every snow season, thousands of adventure seekers flock to Chamonix in France, a picturesque valley surrounded by jagged mountain peaks. Chamonix is the birthplace of extreme skiing. Skiers can ride Europe's highest cable car to over 3,800 meters (12,470 feet) before making the breathtaking descent to the valley floor below.

Snowboarding at Jackson Hole in the United States

Xtreme Fact

The small province of Andorra, in the Pyrénées mountains of Spain, offers quality skiing. The region has a high annual snowfall. A number of resorts have steep grades and top-to-bottom runs for skiers and snowboarders.

Skiing in North America

The Rocky Mountains are home to many of North America's best snow regions, among them:

- ☞ **Whistler, Big White and Fernie in Canada**
- ☞ **Aspen, Telluride and Jackson Hole in the United States.**

An abundance of deep powder snow is a feature of Canada's resorts. In the crisp mountain air of Fernie, the average snowfall of 875 centimeters (28 feet) each season entices many eager skiers and boarders.

WILD AND UNTAMED TERRAIN IN WYOMING

Jackson Hole, Wyoming is considered to be the extreme snowboarding capital of the United States. The terrain is wild and untamed, and is sure to push even the best riders to their limits. The runs are long and steep, and challenges abound at every turn. There is very little flat ground at Jackson Hole. It is an endless procession of cliffs, chutes, rocks and ridges.

Night skiing in Japan

Icy winter storms from Siberia blow across Japan's northernmost island, Hokkaido. Some of the deepest powder snow in the world is dumped onto the Hokkaido snowfields. Night skiing is popular there. Thousands of lights strung in the tree branches illuminate the trails.

Gear Up for the SNOW

BEING PREPARED FOR THE UNEXPECTED

The weather on the slopes can vary a great deal. A day's skiing may begin in bright sunshine, but could easily take a turn for the worse as temperatures suddenly drop and icy winds begin to blow. Skiers and boarders should dress accordingly and always be prepared for the unexpected.

CHOOSING CLOTHING FOR EASE OF MOVEMENT

Traditionally, skiers dressed differently to boarders. Snowboarding requires a wider, crouching stance, and board riders favored a looser style of clothing to allow ease of movement. Today, fans of the two sports tend to wear clothing much more similar in style. A wide range of clothing suitable for both skiing and boarding has become popular.

Snowboarders wear loose clothing for ease of movement.

Wearing Thermals

Thermals, the inner layer of clothing, must be 'breathable'. This type of fabric traps warm air next to the body, yet allows body moisture to escape through the fabric, so that the skier remains comfortable and dry. A fleecy middle layer also provides comfort and warmth.

DRESSING IN LAYERS

The main purpose of snow gear is to keep the body warm and dry. Clothing should allow plenty of freedom for unrestricted movement to ride the bumps and carve huge turns. Many believe it is wise to dress in layers, rather than in a single heavy garment. This allows the skier to peel off a layer if they get hot, or add one if they feel cold.

Xtreme Fact

Skiers stranded by bad weather in the *backcountry*, have a much better chance of surviving if they wear woollen or synthetic thermal underwear. It takes the moisture away from the skin and retains warmth. Cotton becomes damp and retains moisture, lowering the body temperature.

PROTECTING THE HEAD

Much body heat can be lost through the head, so a knit hat or other form of headwear is essential. For extreme skiing and boarding, skiers wear a light, shock-absorbent helmet.

GLOSSARY

backcountry – the natural snow-covered terrain that lies distant from the ski resort

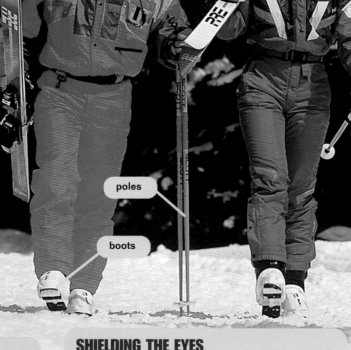

skis

waterproof outerwear

headwear for warmth

waterproof gloves or mittens

poles

boots

CHOOSING COMFORTABLE BOOTS AND BINDINGS

Skiers and boarders alike rely heavily on their boots and bindings to hold their legs securely in position. Boots must be comfortable, and must keep the feet warm and dry. Boot technology varies to suit the needs of different users. Some people prefer quite rigid boots that hold the legs firmly in place when racing or executing sharp turns. Others like some flexibility, to allow the feet to flex and sense the edge of the ski or board.

KEEPING THE HANDS WARM

Tough, waterproof gloves or mittens protect the hands from the cold and wet. They also provide protection from any direct contact with ice or snow. Some people prefer gloves because they allow the fingers to grip better, but others wear mittens for the extra warmth they provide.

Waterproof material on the outside

The jacket and pants, or outerwear, need to be waterproof. Conditions in the snow can be very wet. Outerwear must protect the skier from the cold and strong winds. Underarm vents in the jackets can allow perspiration to escape.

SHIELDING THE EYES

Goggles are vital in protecting the eyes from wind and glare. They allow clear visibility in all weather conditions, and resist fogging. Fogging can be dangerous when skiing or boarding close to others or near hazards such as exposed rocks or treacherous cornices.

Safety in the Snow

Being aware of the risks

Despite the fun you might have in the snow, you need to be aware at all times of the risks you face on the slopes. Hazards are all around. It is a sad fact that many serious injuries, and even deaths, have resulted from snow sports.

Using common sense

Although mishaps do occur, a little common sense when skiing or snowboarding would prevent many of them. Many of the dangers skiers and boarders face result from inadequate preparation, poor technique, failure to observe signs or, unfortunately, the stupidity of others.

Being well prepared

Good preparation includes:

- **checking that all of your clothing and equipment is in good order**
- **taking the time to find out weather and snow conditions before venturing onto the snowfields.**

It is essential that you check the difficulty grading on any ski run or trail when planning to ski or ride in unfamiliar terrain. Seek expert advice about any potential hazards you may encounter.

Staying within your limits

Many accidents occur because skiers and boarders become impatient and try to tackle runs that require greater ability than they possess. It is vital that you learn the basics before you attempt anything too challenging. If you are always able to stay in control, you will be able to avoid colliding with trees, rocks and other skiers and boarders. Stay alert and look ahead. The faster you go, the further ahead you must look.

The ski patroller's job is to warn people of possible dangers and to perform rescue operations.

DANGER

EXTREMELY STEEP SLOPES BEYOND THIS POINT A FALL MAY RESULT IN DEATH

This skier may have eyes on the back of his head, but even he needs to read the signs! Be aware of the risks and obey the signs.

Obeying the signs

All snow sports lovers must learn to read the signs around them. Ski patrols post these signs to warn people of potential hazards. They clearly mark the boundaries of runs and trails considered to be safe. Thrillseekers who venture beyond these bounds in search of untracked powder snow and challenging terrain must be aware of the risks involved in doing this, and must be well prepared to deal with them.

Watching for natural hazards

Nature posts many signs of its own. Consider changing weather conditions as a signal that it is time to leave the slopes and seek shelter. Hard, packed snow or ice may be very slippery underfoot, and could result in a nasty fall.

Cornices on the tops of ridges can be quite unstable, and may break off far back from their edges. They should be avoided when skiing or boarding. Backcountry skiers and riders must be on the lookout for potential avalanche paths. These are places where gravity and other factors can suddenly bring the snowpack crashing down from the side of a mountain. Cross avalanche paths in single file.

Avoiding others on the slopes

The most avoidable accident in the snow is collision with another skier or snowboarder. A few simple rules should take care of this. All skiers and riders are responsible for avoiding those below them. If you want to go fast, stay away from areas of heavy traffic. You may fear the consequences of causing yourself an injury in the snow, but you will feel much worse if you inflict one on someone else.

THE SNURFER

In the winter of 1965, Sherman Poppen, an American, watched his daughter as she struggled to stand up on her sled while riding it down a hill. It gave him an idea. Poppen joined together two children's skis with dowel, and fashioned a type of surfboard for the snow. His daughter was delighted as she rode her new 'Snurfer', as her mother cleverly named it, down the hill. When other children saw it they wanted one too, and soon Poppen was building Snurfers for others.

THE WORLD'S FIRST SNOWBOARD

Poppen had unwittingly invented the world's first snowboard. His Snurfer quickly became popular, and within ten years more than a million were sold in the United States. The Snurfer craze soon spread to Europe.

Design improvements

Early snowboards went through many design changes. For a while, riders steered using fins attached to the base. Jake Burton Carpenter attached adjustable foot straps, and suddenly riders had greater control. Snowboard technology continued to develop at a rapid pace. Today's boards are high-tech devices constructed mainly of strong but thin layers of wood and fibreglass.

Rivalry between skiers and boarders

Among the people initially drawn to snowboarding were surfers, who likened it to riding a wave. Skateboarders could also perform many of their favorite spins and tricks equally well on the snowboard. Soon, a great rivalry developed on the ski slopes between the conservative skiers and the rebellious snowboarders who had introduced a completely new culture to the mountains. They seemed to show no fear at all.

SNOWBOARDING

Snowboarders love to carve huge arcs in fresh powder snow.

Xtreme Fact

In 1999, Australian snowboarder Darren Powell became the world speedboard champion at Les Arcs in France. He notched up a run timed at 201.9 kilometers (125 miles) per hour.

Harmony on the ski runs

There is no longer a great divide between the two snow sports. Snowboarders and skiers accept that there are many similarities between their sports. They each love nothing better than racing at speed down a slope, or carving huge arcs in fresh powder snow. Many skiers have become converts to snowboarding. Recent developments in the technology of each sport have benefited the other. For example, shaped skis borrowed an idea from snowboard design, allowing skiers to carve like boarders. Clothing designs now also suit both sports.

Boarders outnumber skiers

Snowboarding is growing so rapidly that boarders may soon outnumber skiers at resorts. Its huge popularity has spread to all age groups. Almost anyone can now go to a resort, take a few lessons from expert instructors and be carving turns within days.

Learn to link a few turns

Decide on which stance you favor. Once you are able to transfer your weight to put pressure on different parts of the board, you will be able to turn. When you can link a few turns and make your way smoothly down the slope, there will be no stopping you. You can really start to enjoy yourself on increasingly steeper and bumpier slopes as your confidence and control grows, and your speed increases. Soon you will be carving and **taking air** with the best of them.

Freeriding or freestyle?

Freeriding, the downhill form of the sport, is the most widespread form of snowboarding. Freestyle is the form of snowboarding in which tricks are performed. It features spectacular aerial stunts, usually performed on the **halfpipe**. Snowboarding now enjoys the status of being a Winter Olympic sport.

The moves

Freeriding is the most common form of snowboarding.
The main features of freeriding include:

- ☛ speeding fearlessly down steep alpine slopes
- ☛ skillfully carving graceful arcs with the edge of your board in deep powder snow
- ☛ leaning way over on the turns
- ☛ experiencing the sheer exhilaration of the descent.

A versatile board

The freeriding board is the most versatile of boards. It is often longer and thinner than the freestyle board. Because it is generally the same shape at each end, the board can be turned around and ridden with either foot forward. The most common stance is with the left foot forward, but some prefer to ride **goofy**, leading with their right foot. A quality freeriding board will allow you to ride wherever your sense of adventure takes you. You can ride it through deep powder, down icy steep slopes, in and out of a row of trees, and even over cliffs.

Freeriders enjoy the freedom of being able to speed down steep slopes found well away from crowded ski resorts.

Steep backcountry slopes

There is nothing a freerider loves more than a steep backcountry mountain slope with a thick carpet of fresh, untracked powder snow. In order to find such snow, you may have to trek well away from the crowded runs of a resort and, of course, the safety of nearby ski patrols.

THE CHALLENGE

It is often this element of risk that motivates an extreme rider. The knowledge that, without warning, the weather could suddenly turn nasty, or that an unsighted rock or cliff may suddenly present itself is what brings on the adrenalin rush. The challenge is knowing when to tackle the danger head-on and when to ease off.

Freeriding

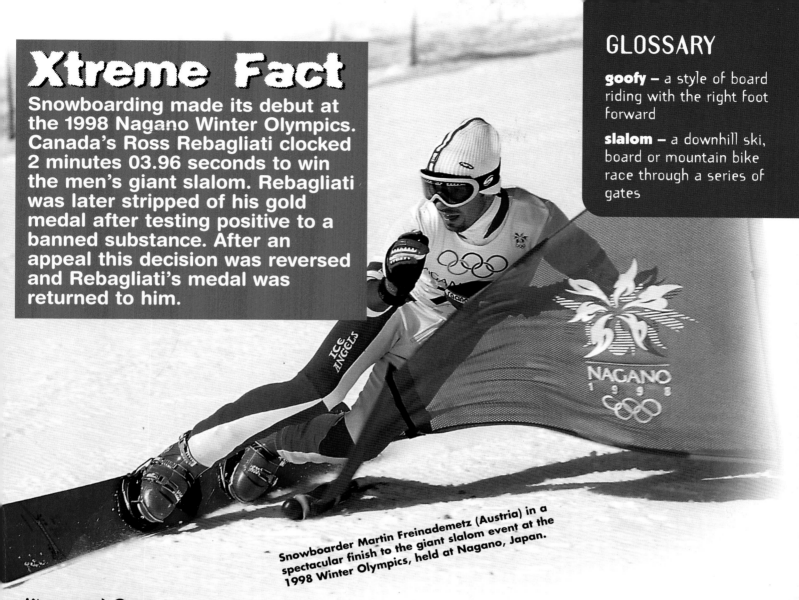

Xtreme Fact

Snowboarding made its debut at the 1998 Nagano Winter Olympics. Canada's Ross Rebagliati clocked 2 minutes 03.96 seconds to win the men's giant slalom. Rebagliati was later stripped of his gold medal after testing positive to a banned substance. After an appeal this decision was reversed and Rebagliati's medal was returned to him.

Snowboarder Martin Freinademetz (Austria) in a spectacular finish to the giant slalom event at the 1998 Winter Olympics, held at Nagano, Japan.

King and Queen of the Hill

Some extreme riders compete in races such as the King and Queen of the Hill, which is the World Championships of snowboarding. This competition is held annually in Alaska, in the Chugach Mountains surrounding Valdez. Competitors are transported to the top of the course by helicopter, then race against the clock as they hurtle down the steepest of slopes at lightning speed.

A DEMANDING TRAINING SCHEDULE

Only the fittest and most fearless snowboarders can match such conditions. In order to be the best in the world, these elite athletes undertake a demanding training schedule that usually includes weights training, cycling and running. They also need plenty of practice on the board.

RACING GEAR

Racing, or alpine, boards are longer, narrower and stiffer than conventional freeriding boards. They go very fast, and are great for carving turns in powder snow. Racers usually prefer hard boots and bindings. These hold their feet firmly in place on the board. Hard boots do not allow the racers to 'feel' the edge of their boards in the way that the soft boots or step-in boots of the freeriders do.

RACING EVENTS

Racing events are usually either the giant **slalom** or the super G. Competitors in slalom events must race the clock as they pass through a series of gates on a marked downhill course. The giant slalom event usually takes place on a course with a vertical drop of between 120 and 300 meters (400 and 1,000 feet) and at least 20 meters (66 feet) in width. Super G races are held on a wider course with a vertical drop of between 300 and 500 meters (1,000 and 1,640 feet).

Freestyle riding

Many snowboarders, especially those with an interest in skateboarding, prefer the gravity defying thrills and spills of freestyle riding. Freestyle boarding has become so popular that many resorts now construct snowboard parks as a challenging alternative to the regular downhill runs. These parks feature natural terrain with steep slopes, bumps and gullies, along with areas where obstacles such as rails, tables and even buried cars have been placed for riders to slide across or jump over.

SLOPE STYLE

There are two disciplines of freestyle riding: slope style and halfpipe. Slope style boarders perform as many different tricks as possible on the slope, by jumping over a series of natural and human-made obstacles. These include bumps, rails and other objects. Some riders compete in big air contests, jumping off specially built mounds of snow in spectacular displays of aerial acrobatics.

HALFPIPE ACTION

A highlight of the snowboard park is the halfpipe, a long, U-shaped, snow-covered ramp with opposing curved walls about 3.5 meters (11.5 feet) in height. Riders travel back and forth from wall to wall along the pipes, taking air and performing tricks. Many of these tricks are adapted from skateboarding, and are used by skilled riders to display their individual style. They include **grabs**, spins and flips.

THE OLLIE

One of the first freestyle tricks to learn is the **ollie**. This is a way to use your own energy to jump the board and land again. It is a fun trick that can help you get over small obstacles as a beginner. As your skills improve, you may use it to get up on rails and other obstacles.

Freestyle snowboarding – slope style

Freestyle and Boardercross

Boardercross

Boardercross is an exciting form of snowboard racing. It takes place on a course similar to that used for motocross racing. Four, or sometimes six, competitors line up in starting gates behind a wooden boom. When the starter drops the boom, the riders burst out of the gates, using the steep slope to gain as much speed as possible.

A CHALLENGING COURSE

The boardercross course features a series of left- and right-hand turns, with a number of obstacles in between. The corners of the turns are sloped embankments called **berms**. The slope allows you to take the turns at high speed, and then to accelerate out of the turn in the new direction. Between the

GLOSSARY

grab – a freestyle trick where the rider grabs the board or ski while airborne

ollie – a snowboarding trick in which the rider uses his or her own energy to jump the board

berms – sloped embankments placed on the turn of boardercross or Biker X courses

berms lie whoopdy-doos and tabletops. Whoopdy-doos are a series of two or three mounds of snow placed close together, just a few feet apart. Tabletops are larger jumps, often positioned where spectators will get the best view as the riders take air. Because you travel faster on snow than in the air, avoid jumping too high or staying airborne for too long.

ROUGH CORNERS

As you tackle the racing course, you not only have to overcome the obstacles in your way, but also jostle each other to get the best position. Some competitors try to break away to an early lead, because it gets fairly rough on the corners when several riders arrive at the same time, often resulting in falls. Helmets are essential in this event.

A GROWING SPORT

Boardercross has gained many fans, and now has its own world tour. Top professional boardercross riders travel between events, conducting demonstrations, competing for prize money and promoting their sponsors' products.

Competition is fierce in the 1998 boardercross event at the 1998 Winter X Games. Crested Butte, Rocky Mountains, USA.

Xtreme Fact

Perhaps the greatest freestyle snowboarder ever is Norway's Terje Haakonsen. His halfpipe dominance began in 1992, with victories at the US Open and the World Cup. Since then, Haakonsen has continued to win a number of world and national titles.

EXTREME SKIING

In the 1970s, the term 'extreme skiing' was coined to describe a group of courageous French skiers who liked to climb high, remote mountains with steep slopes and then ski down them. Within a short time, American skiers had taken up the challenge of steep descents, hurtling down the mountainsides at even greater speeds than the Europeans. Many of these extreme skiing pioneers were also highly skilled **mountaineers**. A skier usually had to complete a difficult, sometimes dangerous, climb to reach the summit first.

Free skiers take downhill skiing to the absolute limit on steep mountain slopes.

introducing the world to extreme skiing

By the early 1980s, film-makers such as Warren Miller began to show the world what extreme skiing was all about. Miller had made his first ski film in 1949, and continued to produce one each season for the following fifty years. He introduced the world to a new group of skiers who jumped off cliffs, displaying remarkable aerial skills as they plunged several feet to the steep powder slopes below.

SKI MOUNTAINEERS

Today, those skiers who prefer to combine the arduous climb to the top with a thrilling descent down the mountain are generally known as 'ski mountaineers'. 'Free skiing' became the popular term used to describe all other forms of extreme downhill skiing. Many free skiers prefer quicker and easier access to the summit, using **snowcats** and helicopters to reach remote slopes, where they have hundreds of vertical feet of untracked powder snow all to themselves.

SKIING TO THE LIMIT

Free skiers take downhill skiing to the absolute limit. They plough through deep powder, carve big turns and take air over bumps and cliffs. They ski steep, long lines down the mountainside, always at the very edge of control.

Sidecut skis

Until recently, skis had long parallel sides. Ski designers began to experiment with the shape of the skis by shortening the length and curving in the sides at the center to produce an elongated 'hourglass' shape. This sidecut, as the change in width is known, allows more of the ski's edge to stay in contact with the snow. Free skiing benefited greatly from the introduction of these shaped skis. Skiers found it much easier to carve big turns and, importantly, to remain in control on the steepest slopes.

Free skiing locations

Today, some of the most spectacular mountains around the globe that attract daredevil free skiers are:

- ☛ **European Alps**
- ☛ **North American Rocky Mountains**
- ☛ **South American Andes**
- ☛ **Alpine regions of southern Australia and New Zealand.**

HELI-SKIING IN NEW ZEALAND

A number of international free skiing events have evolved. At Wanaka, in the Southern Alps of New Zealand, an annual three-day challenge draws together the world's most daring free skiers. They ride helicopters to previously inaccessible mountain peaks, then attempt to score the most points by skiing down the slopes in the most stylish, yet challenging, way they can.

THE ULTIMATE FREE SKIING CHALLENGE

Perhaps the greatest challenge for free skiers lies in the Chugach Mountains that surround the port of Valdez in Alaska. Here, in the Thompson Pass area, icy winds often reach 160 kilometers (100 miles) per hour. More than 1,000 centimeters (32.5 feet) of snow falls every year. Fresh, untracked powder snow drops away to the valley floor a mile or more below, presenting the ultimate challenge for the free skier.

Xtreme Fact

Film-maker Warren Miller and his team travelled about 192,000 kilometers (119,300 miles) in search of the perfect free skiing run for the movie *Freeriding*. In doing so, they skied a world record of 107,800 vertical meters (67,000 feet) in a single day.

Gaining access to some of the most remote areas via helicopter provides free skiers with plenty of powder snow and thrilling slopes to conquer.

Touchdown in the Chugachs

March and April are the best times of year to ski at Valdez. Fresh, soft snow covers the mountains from top to bottom and, if the sun is shining, conditions could never be better. There is not a tree in sight as a helicopter touches down lightly near the pinnacle in the Chugach range.

Take in the majestic mountains

The view from the summit is awesome. Great snowy peaks rise in all directions. Stretching out before the skier is a mountain slope so steep, with powder so fresh and deep, it almost takes your breath away.

Wait for the right moment

Examine the route you will follow to the valley below. Try to 'read' the snow as a fisherman might read the mood of the sea. You may have to spend several anxious days holed up in a Valdez hotel, waiting for the fierce wind to stop blowing and the skies to clear. Closely observe the way the snow lies on the mountainside. If you make a wrong decision and ski before the snow is ready, you risk being buried under tons of snow in an avalanche. Even the best free skiers know it is wise to return home and live to ski another day if conditions are not right.

Begin the descent

Any doubts will be banished from your mind as you begin the descent. Your speed accelerates as you apply pressure to the edges of your skis and begin carving large, graceful turns deep in the snow. Nothing could be better than this!

Every April, the world's best skiers and snowboarders travel to the majestic Chugach mountains in Alaska, to compete in the King and Queen of the Hill events.

Focus ahead

Try not to look too far down the hill. Your eyes should be focused just a little way ahead to where you will land your next turn. Your speed will be so great that several feet pass by in split seconds.

Think quickly and use your instincts

When free skiing be prepared for whatever might suddenly appear in your path. You might suddenly reach a big, snowy cliff and, moments later, might be dropping 20 meters (66 feet) through the air, preparing to land. Rocky patches appear and you begin an unexpected series of high-speed turns to skillfully navigate between them. Quick thinking and natural instincts are all that you can rely on at this stage. Learn to anticipate the hazards you may encounter.

Push even harder

When the obstacles are safely behind you, the terrain becomes steeper and the snow lies like a vast white carpet over the slope. You gain confidence and push your body even harder than before, taking in every exhilarating moment as you race on towards the rapidly approaching valley floor. Behind you lie deep curving tracks in the snow.

Participate in world championships

Each April, the world's best free skiers and snowboarders travel to the Chugachs to contest the King and Queen of the Hill events for men and women. These events are the world championships of the two sports. They provide spectacular television entertainment for thousands of viewers. Competitors attempt to take the most challenging line of descent in the fastest possible time. As difficult as it may be, the skiers must remain in control at all times.

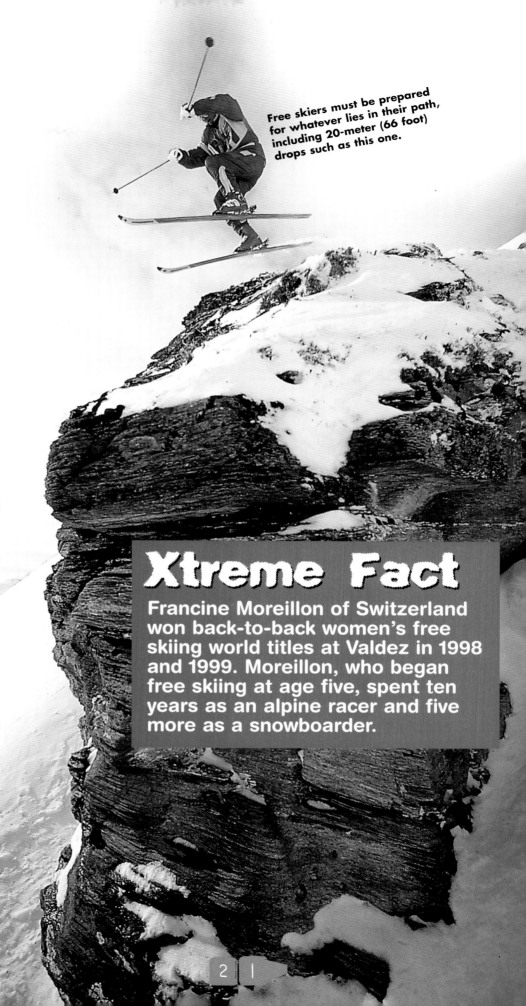

Free skiers must be prepared for whatever lies in their path, including 20-meter (66 foot) drops such as this one.

Xtreme Fact

Francine Moreillon of Switzerland won back-to-back women's free skiing world titles at Valdez in 1998 and 1999. Moreillon, who began free skiing at age five, spent ten years as an alpine racer and five more as a snowboarder.

SKIBOARDING

A NEW WAY TO ENJOY THE SNOW

For many years, traditional alpine skiing dominated the ski slopes — until the introduction of the snowboard offered people an exciting alternative. Snowboarding grew in popularity, developing its own culture and attracting many converts from regular skiing. Snow sports lovers continued to look for new ways to enjoy the snow.

Christopher Hawks takes air during the skiboarding event at the 1998 Winter X Games. Crested Butte, Rocky Mountains, USA.

BIG FOOT

In the early 1990s, a new type of ski was developed. It was a very short ski, just 63 centimeters (2 feet) in length. It was named Big Foot, after the mythical creature that was said to roam the forests of North America. Big Foot's designer gave it **sidecut** and toes so that it did actually resemble a rather large foot.

THE NEED FOR A BETTER SHORT SKI

Many people tried Big Foot for the novelty of riding such small skis. Few riders attempted to push these skis to the limits, because they were not really built for that purpose. Some, however, saw the possibilities for a short ski, and went to work to develop a better model.

THE SKIBOARD

A number of design changes throughout the 1990s resulted in a ski measuring about 90 centimeters (35 inches). This ski was lightweight and symmetrical in shape, with twin tips allowing it to travel forwards, backwards or sideways with ease. Resembling a cross between a small ski and a snowboard, it was named the 'skiboard'. Bindings suitable for both ski boots and snowboard boots were added. This allowed riders to step in and attach their boards without using their hands.

Skiboarding as a sport

Skiboarding soon grew in popularity, in much the same way that snowboarding had done some years earlier. Skiboarding rapidly developed from being simply a form of recreation to an organized sport. Major skiboarding events were established, and skiboard manufacturers began to sponsor riders. Thirty thousand skiboards were sold across the United States in the winter of 1996–97, the sport's first official season. The following year, 350,000 skiboard sales were recorded. In 1998, skiboarding made its debut at the Winter X Games, held in Crested Butte, Colorado. Skiboarding had well and truly arrived on the slopes.

EASY TO LEARN

One possible reason for the rapid growth of skiboarding is the short time it takes to learn the basic movements. Most people move with good control within an hour or two of their first lesson. Most beginning skiboarders are able to master moderately difficult terrain by only their third run down the mountain. By comparison, it often takes months to become a competent alpine skier.

SKIBOARDING IN THE MEDIA

Another possible reason the sport blossomed is the extensive media coverage it gained over a short period of time. Millions of people watching the evening news saw the UK's Prince Harry having a wonderful time using the short skis on the Swiss Alps. Sensational television coverage of the Winter X Games gave viewers a sampling of the many exciting tricks a skiboarder could perform.

GLOSSARY

sidecut – the change in width in a shaped ski, which is narrower at the center than at either end

Skiboarding at the Winter X Games, Crested Butte, Colorado.

Xtreme Fact

Jason Levinthal designed the first twin-tip skiboards. By the age of 24 he had established his home-based company, Line Skiboards, and produced enough boards to take the ski industry by storm in the late 1990s.

Skiboard fun

INDEPENDENT LEG ACTION

Skiboarding has become the favorite winter sport of many inline skaters and skateboarders. Skiboard riders use a leg action similar to that used by inline skaters. Each leg moves independently of the other on the short skiboards. Skateboarders enjoy the sport because they can slide forwards, backwards or sideways in much the same way that they ride their boards on the street. They can also carve big turns and perform similar aerial tricks with both types of gear. Balance and control are essential elements of each sport.

Other uses for skiboards

Sometimes regular skiers turn to skiboards as tools to help them develop the fine balance and carving skills they need to use with longer skis. If there is deep powder on the slopes, longer skis are less effective because of their tendency to sink into the snow. Skiboards do not weigh much and can be used in many different ways. Some mountaineers use slightly longer models for hiking into the challenging terrain of the backcountry.

AERIAL ACTION

Some of the best fun riders have with skiboards is at snowboard parks. Here the jumps, rails and halfpipes provide opportunities to perform aerial tricks that are simply not possible with skis and longer boards. New skiboard tricks are being developed all the time, since the sport is still quite new. Many tricks are adapted from skateboarding.

Skiboard tricks

Flips feature prominently in skiboarding. There are few sights more spectacular than a rider accelerating towards a snow jump, taking off, somersaulting gracefully through a full rotation and landing with perfect poise and balance. Backflips can be even more dramatic.

SPECTACULAR SPINS

Spins are also popular. They generally take their names from the number of degrees turned. For example, a rider who spins around once in the air and lands facing in the same direction has turned through a full circle of 360 degrees. This trick is known as a '360'. A rider who spins through half a circle and lands facing backwards, or **fakie**, has performed a '180'. It is not uncommon to see the world's best riders perform 720s or even 1080s in competition.

COMBINED MOVES

Some tricks combine flips and spins. A corkscrew is a sideways front flip with a 180-degree twist and a backward landing. Other skiboarding tricks are also known by interesting names. A trick in which the rider adopts a cross-legged sitting position while in the air is called a Yoda, after the character from the *Star Wars* movies. A Sock-Eyed Salmon is a front grab with a twist, resembling the motion of the fish as it leaps and twists when reaching a small waterfall.

THE GRIND AND SLIDE

You do not always have to take air to have fun with a skiboard. Like the skateboard, skiboards can be used to grind or slide down handrails and tabletops buried in the snow. The Triple Air competition is an event that combines the rider's skill in negotiating a challenging course with their ability to take air and perform tricks. This event displays skiboarding talent at its finest.

Xtreme Fact

Mike Nick from the USA won the skiboard freestyle gold medal at the Winter X Games, held in Crested Butte in 1998. Nick almost pulled off a 1260 spin (three-and-a-half turns), but lost his footing upon landing.

England's Prince Harry at Klosters ski resort in Switzerland, 1998.

WINTER X GAMES

Television coverage of the Winter X Games brings all the excitement of extreme snow sports to millions of fans around the world. Year after year, as the event grows, more and more new sports are introduced. Snow mountain biking is one such sport. It is still rarely performed outside competition events.

SPEED EVENT

Riders in the speed event hurtle down the mountain on studded tires. They often reach speeds in excess of 115 kilometers (71 miles) per hour. These riders wear skintight suits made of high-tech fabric designed to reduce wind resistance. However, these suits are so slippery that if riders fall they may find it impossible to stop if they ever make contact with the snow. Helmets are also necessary protection from serious injury during such a mishap. Riders sometimes need to place their feet on the ground to bring their bikes to a gradual halt at the bottom of a hill. Brakes can be quite ineffective on the ice and snow.

DUAL DOWNHILL EVENT

When snow mountain biking first made its appearance late in the 1990s, there were two X Games events, the dual downhill race and the speed race. The dual downhill event pits two riders against each other in a race to the finish line. They hunch down low over their bikes and pedal furiously down a steep slope, weaving in and out of slalom gates. Cornering is tough, because riders have to work against the downhill momentum of their bikes while they battle to maintain control as they round each of the markers.

SNOW MOUNTAIN BIKING

New conditions

The first Winter X Games events featured contestants from among the world's best mountain bikers. Some of them had never even been to the snow before. Few knew quite what to expect from their first experience of riding on snow. However, most of the competitors were talented bike riders and had vast experience in riding through mud and slush in all types of weather. Most were able to adapt remarkably well to the conditions after a few trial runs.

It takes about four hours to drill the studs into each tire.

studs

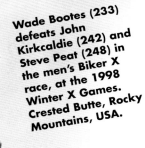

Wade Bootes (233) defeats John Kirkcaldie (242) and Steve Peat (248) in the men's Biker X race, at the 1998 Winter X Games. Crested Butte, Rocky Mountains, USA.

Studded tires

The riders fitted their bikes with metal studs, up to 400 in each tire. This helped them gain traction in the snow.

Most snow mountain bikers prefer to ride on ice rather than on soft, fresh snow. Fresh snow makes the course slow and slippery. Studded tires are not as effective on soft snow as they are on an icier surface. If snow does not fall on the night before a race, the course is usually slick and fast, which is how the riders like it best.

A change in format

As the Winter X Games evolved, snow mountain biking competitors suggested a change in the format of their events. The dual downhill and speed events were dropped in favor of Biker X, an exciting but hazardous form of racing that closely resembles boardercross and BMX racing. A new form of downhill race was developed, where four riders race in each heat. This event was introduced at the first Australian Winter X Games, held at Perisher, New South Wales in 1999.

Xtreme Fact

Entrants in the Winter X Games snow mountain biking events usually excel in either mountain biking or BMX. The winner of the 1997 women's Winter X dual speed event, Cheri Elliot of the USA, also happened to be national off-road downhill champion and the only woman in the BMX Hall of Fame.

AN IMMEDIATE HIT

Biker X was introduced at the 1999 Winter X Games, held at Crested Butte, Colorado. It was an immediate hit with spectators.

A punishing downhill course

Six riders compete in each Biker X heat. The first three finishers from each heat advance to the next round, and slower riders are eliminated. Eventually, only six riders remain to contest the final. Their aim is to be first across the finish line at the end of a punishing downhill course. The course is about 300 meters (1,000 feet) in length, and consists of a series of tight, banked turns and challenging jumps.

A frantic scramble on the turns

The six riders line up behind a starting gate at the top of the course. Their immediate goal is to get away to a fast start, and to create a gap between themselves and the rest of the pack. Once a clear lead is established, the rider must strive to maintain it. The leader must try not to get caught up in the tangle of elbows and wheels coming from behind. Often there is mayhem as four or five riders scramble into a turn at the same time, resulting in spectacular collisions.

Courage and common sense

The banked turns, or berms, are often treacherous. If the riders do not slow down and approach the berms with caution, they can easily lose control and collide with others. Since all riders attempt to take a similar line through the course at speeds of over 70 kilometers (43 miles) per hour, Biker X demands both courage and common sense.

A wise rider may actually ease off on the approach to a turn, allowing the rest of the field to surge ahead into the berm. This is the best way to avoid a collision.

Tara Llanes (276) defeats Elke Brutsaert (268, third) and Missy Giove (274, fourth) in the women's Biker X race, at the 1998 Winter X Games, Crested Butte, USA.

Biker X

The hazards of snow mountain biking

Collisions are frequent, and can have a dramatic effect on the race. Some riders are able to remount their bikes and continue the race. Others are not so lucky. In the 1999 women's X Games final, half of the competitors did not make it to the finish line. Only the winner, Tara Llanes, came through without being involved in any crashes, though even she suffered the indignity of ripping her pants on her spiked rear tire. It is not uncommon for a rider's legs to suffer cuts and bruises through accidental contact with the sharp studs of another rider's tire.

BIG AIR

In addition to the treacherous turns, the course features a number of impressive snow jumps. Mountain bikers generally enjoy the opportunity to take big air over a jump, but this can be a risky decision. Sometimes, when a rider becomes airborne from a double jump, a rival may attempt to stay closer to the ground and speed past. This tricky maneuver can also result in a tangle of bikes.

The ultimate adrenaline rush

There are thrills and spills aplenty in the new action sport of Biker X. Snow mountain biking combines speed and daring with physical contact, aerial stunts and tactical skill. It provides the ultimate adrenaline rush for competitor and spectator alike.

Xtreme Fact

Steve Peat, winner of the men's Biker X at the 1999 Winter X Games, was last out of the gate and fourth at the first turn. One of the leaders went for big air off the double jump, but landed too quickly to take the second turn. Peat sped past and was never headed again.

Snow Jargon

bust a huge turn
to carve a wide arc through powder snow
> "I was busting huge turns all the way to the bottom."

crowd-pleaser
a spectacular trick
> "Her last aerial trick off the halfpipe was a real crowd-pleaser."

drop in
to successfully complete an aerial maneuver from a cliff
> "It takes a lot of courage to drop in like she just did."

freshies
plenty of fresh powder snow
> "I was hoping Mother Nature would give us some freshies overnight."

gnarly
awesome; really challenging
> "Conditions were gnarly for backcountry skiing today."

grommet
the youngest skier or snowboarder in a group
> "I learned lots of new tricks when I was a grommet."

huckfest
a snowboarding session where everyone recklessly tries to take bigger air than the other members of the group — can be quite hazardous
> "We spent the afternoon on the halfpipe, taking part in a huge huckfest."

inverted
upside down
> "I tried to nail a few inverted stunts off the halfpipe."

kicker
a large snow jump
> "He hit a huge kicker and took big air."

nose/tail grab
a trick in which the nose or tail of the board is grabbed while jumping
> "As he came off the kicker he pulled a tail grab."

rolling down the windows
flailing the arms in an attempt to stay upright and balanced
> "He was rolling down the windows as he lost control over the jump."

shifty
swivelling the hips to the side while taking air on a jump
> "I hung a shifty as I left the kicker."

stoked
ecstatic; really pleased
> "She was absolutely stoked when she nailed that last trick."

Glossary

adrenaline rush
the special feeling that accompanies a thrilling experience

backcountry
the natural, snow-covered terrain that lies distant from the ski resort

berms
sloped embankments placed on the turn of a boardercross or Biker X course

carving
using the edge of the skis or board to cut into the surface of the snow when turning

fakie
riding backwards

goofy
a style of board riding with the right foot forward

grab
a freestyle trick where the rider grabs the board or ski while airborne

halfpipe
a U-shaped, snow-covered ramp with curved walls, used for performing tricks with a snowboard or skiboards

mountaineers
people who climb mountains

ollie
a snowboard trick in which the rider uses his or her own energy to jump the board

powder
soft, fresh snow

resorts
usually villages with groomed ski runs serviced by a lift system

sidecut
the change in width in a shaped ski, which is narrower at the center than at either end

slalom
a downhill ski, board or mountain bike race through a series of gates

snowcats
powerful, motorized snow vehicles used to transport skiers

taking air
a jump or leap

terrain
the natural features of the land

trail
an area of groomed, skiable snow with marked boundaries

Index

A
air 4, 6, 7, 8, 13, 16, 17, 18, 21, 25, 29, 30
Andorra (Spain) 7
Australia 6, 13, 19, 27
    Thredbo 6
avalanches 11, 20

B
berms 17
Big Foot, 22
Biker X *see* snow mountain biking
bindings 9, 15
boardercross *see* snowboarding
Bootes, Wade 27
boots 9, 15, 22
Brutsaert, Elke 28

C
Canada
    Fernie 7
Carpenter, Jake Burton 12
carving 4, 8, 13, 14, 15, 18, 19, 20, 24
Chugach Mountains, Alaska 15, 19, 20, 21
clothing 8, 9, 10–11, 13

D
dangers 10–11

E
Elliot, Cheri 27
equipment 8–9, 10
Europe 7, 12, 18, 19
European Alps 7
extreme skiing, *see* free skiing

F
France 7, 13, 18
    Chamonix 7
free riding *see* snowboarding
free skiing 4, 6, 18, 19, 20, 21
freestyle *see* snowboarding

G
Giove, Missy 28

H
Haakonsen, Terje 17
halfpipe 13, 16, 24
Heli-Challenge 6
heli-skiing 6, 18, 19

I
inline skating 5, 24

J
Japan 7

K
King of the Hill 15, 20, 21
Kirkcalder, James 27

L
Levinthal, Jason 23
Llanes, Tara 28, 29

M
Miller, Warren 18
Moreillon, Francine 21
mountain biking 27
mountaineers 18, 24

N
New Zealand
    Wanaka 6, 19
night skiing 7

O
ollie 16

P
Peat, Steve 27, 29
Poppen, Sherman 12
Powell, Darren 13
Prince Harry 23

Q
Queen of the Hill 15, 20, 21

R
Rocky Mountains 5, 7

S
safety 5, 10, 11, 14
skateboarding 12, 16, 24, 25
ski resorts 4, 6, 7, 13, 14, 16, 30
skiboarding 5, 22, 23, 24, 25
skiing 4, 5, 6, 7, 8, 9, 10, 11, 12, 13, 18, 19, 20, 21, 22, 23, 24
skis 19, 22
slalom events 15, 26
snow mountain biking 5, 26, 27, 29
    Biker X 17, 27, 28–29, 30
snowboarding 4, 5, 6, 7, 8, 9, 10, 11, 12, 13, 14, 15, 16, 17, 21, 22, 23, 24, 30
    boardercross 16, 17
    freeriding 13, 14, 15
    freestyle 13, 14, 16, 30
snowboards 12–13, 14, 15
snowcats 16, 17
Snowy Mountains 6
Snurfer 12
studded tires 26, 27, 29
Switzerland 7, 23

U
United States of America 7, 12, 18, 19, 23
    Valdez, Alaska 15, 19, 20
    Crested Butte, Colorado 5, 22, 23, 28
    Jackson Hole, Wyoming 7

V
Valdez *see* Chugach Mountains

W
weather 10
whoopdy-doos 17
Winter Olympic Games 5, 13, 15
Winter X Games 5, 17, 22, 23, 26–27, 28, 29
World Cup 17